NELLIE

The Lighthouse dog

Story by Jane Scarpino
Illustrated by Robert Ensor

A Windswept Book

Windswept House Publishers Mount Desert, Maine 04660

Copyright by Jane Scarpino and Robert Ensor 1993
Library of Congress No. 93-060463
ISBN 0-932433-23-5

15 14 13

Printed in the United States of America
for the Publisher by
Downeast Printers and Graphics, Inc.
Ellsworth, Maine 04605

Dedication

To our friends, near and far, who love the
Coast of Maine, and especially Marshall Point.

My name is NELLIE.
I'm a wiry dog with sparkling eyes ~ ~ ~ ~ ~

up

and one ear

and one ear ....

and a ~ ~ ~ ~ ~ ~ flaggy~waggy tail.

down ~

I live in a lovely old house in the small fishing village of PORT CLYDE MAINE. In the summer I lie on the vine-shaded porch ~ with a bowl of fresh water.

Most every day my master takes me to the
Post Office in his car ~ ~ ~ I do like to ride!

When my cousin Gracie comes to visit it's holiday time for her and me.
We play, and get into all kinds of mischief, but no one minds because
we have such a good time. I am so sad when she goes home.

In the winter I have a coat with my name on it, and I can watch the big yellow school bus go by.

SCHOOL DISTRICT NO 50

15

NELLIE
FROM
PORT CLYDE

DOG

©1993 Rob Henson

Just before Christmas my master, mistress and I look for just the right tree. I wear my red coat and he carries a little axe. After it is cut I help drag the tree thru the snow.

A big red engine lives in the firehouse across the street ~ ~
Sometimes men come running to jump onto the engine and off
they go to put out a fire. The siren wails ∘∘∘∘∘ and I howl with it.

When we walk to the beach there are lots of kids splashing and playing~They are having such a good time!One small girl throws me her ball and~of course~I catch it. I like to join in their games.

We often visit Lee's boat shop, where he fixes lobster boats and little dinghies. Sometimes he gives me candy ~ I shouldn't have it ~ but it sure tastes good.

When we walk to the village we go past a spookedy old building back in the trees. It's been deserted for a long time and I'm sure a ghost lives there ~   ~   ~
If you don't mind ~ let's walk F-A-S-T-E-R master.

I am such a lucky dog to get to walk through the village. My doggie friends all greet me "Hi Nellie"-"Good morning Nellie" and I bark back "The same to you-Ginger-Big Ben-Blackie-and the two Jakes."

My eyes sparkle ~ my tail wags ~ Oh Boy! we are at the Ice Cream Shop. "Make mine strawberry please ~ ~ and in a cup."

We stopped by the docks to watch my friend, Allison, unload his boat. He held up a very large lobster and I moved closer to see better. I sure jumped back in a hurry when the big fellow waved his claws at me!

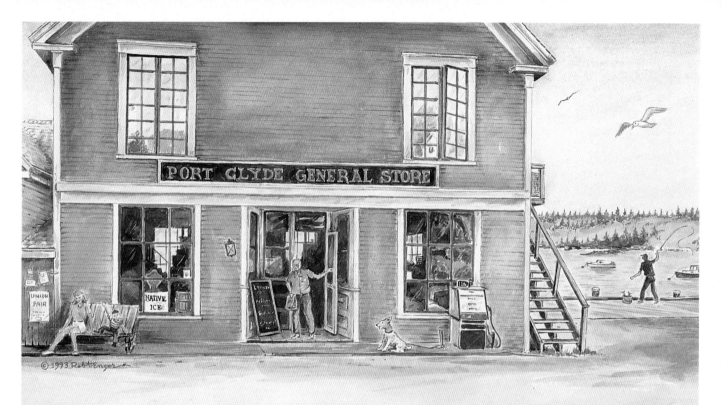

We some times stop at the General Store for some things. I try to be very good so that maybe he will bring me a treat. If there is a newspaper - my job is to carry it.

One day when I was carrying the paper I forgot and barked "Hello" ~ to a friend. The paper fell right into a puddle. I can't repeat what my master said.

But my most fun is the daily walk to MARSHALL POINT. Thats the best walk I know, along the woodsy way, with all the good smells of my wild and furry friends.

Mr. Fred and I are great friends and when we walk past his house he always calls out "Hi Nellie-glad to see you." He has even forgiven me for the time I knocked over his paint and I got paw prints where they should not be.

On the way to the lighthouse we sometimes walk up the driveway to the FIELDSTONE CASTLE to see if the twins, Kamissa and Jonathan, and their dog Emmett are home. I guess not today - - Oh well! - - Maybe next time.

Near the lighthouse there is a brown cottage where two sweet ladies live. Ms. Marion is 96, Ms. Eula is 102. As little girls they lived at the lighthouse where their father was keeper for 45yrs. They watch for me and always wave through the window.

When we reach the lighthouse, there is a museum, where lots of
friendly people pat me, and talk to me. There is also the keeper's kitty,
Puffin. How we like to play, chasing each other ~ round and round.

My master lets me off leash, and I have a great time exploring the rocks. Sometimes there is a baby seal, and always little critters in the tidal pools. One big rock looks like a chair with a cushion ~ big people like to sit there to watch the eider ducks, and the gulls and, of course, the lobster boats.

One sunny day while I was chasing some butterflies over the rocks my floppy ear heard a strange mewing sound. To my stand-up ear, it sounded like someone crying.

"What can this be?" said I to myself and began hopping from rock to rock ~ "HA!" ~ "I found it!" ~ ~

At the bottom of the big chair rock huddled a little boy crying bitterly. I went to him, cocked my head in question and gave him my paw. He put his tear-wet face in my fur ~ and hugged me.

"Oh doggy" he sobbed, "I cannot find my way back to my mother. The rocks are so big, and the waves are rolling, and I can't climb up to see - - - I am really lost."

"Not to worry," I said to myself, and nimbly hopped up on a big rock. Over by the lighthouse walkway, a group of people stood, looking about and calling JOHNNNEE....... JOHNNNEE........ but the wind  was carrying their voices away. I began

to bark and bark and dance around on that rock.

"Look at that foolish dog", someone said, "he's probably found a seal pup - or a gull - but we should go see anyway", - as I kept on barking.

Soon everyone was hugging me and patting my head until I thought both ears would be floppy.

"Good dog, good dog" they said, and my flaggy ~ waggy tail was going fast with happiness, as they made their way back to the museum to wash away ~ little boy's tears, and give him an apple, and some shells to play with.

I sure was the heroine of __THAT__ day! Like the keepers of old I helped someone in distress ~ and ever since then I have been known as ~

NELLIE
The Lighthouse Dog

It makes me very proud.

© 1993 Robt Tenso

THE END

© 1993 Rob Fenson

Robert T. Ensor   Nellie   Jane Scarpino   @ Thomas Mark Szelog

About the Author

Jane H. Scarpino makes her home in Port Clyde, Maine. She and her late husband, Captain H.C. Scarpino were charter members of the Marshall Point Restoration Comittee.

Mother of four, she is now grandmother to girls, dogs and cats.

About the Illustrator

Robert T. Ensor was born and raised in Ohio, where he attended Miami University. He served 27 months in the South Pacific with a combat Engineer Intelligence Section. He worked for 33 years at a Research and Development Company in Connecticut as an instrument design engineer, and also pursued a life long interest in art by painting watercolor landscapes and commercial art work. In 1985 he retired with his wife, Eloise, to their second home in Port Clyde, Maine where Nellie soon joined them. They, and many others, were active on the team that restored the National Historic Site Keepers House for use as the Marshall Point Light-House Museum, where Bob is currently Director.

To visit Nellie's Museum, just follow this map.

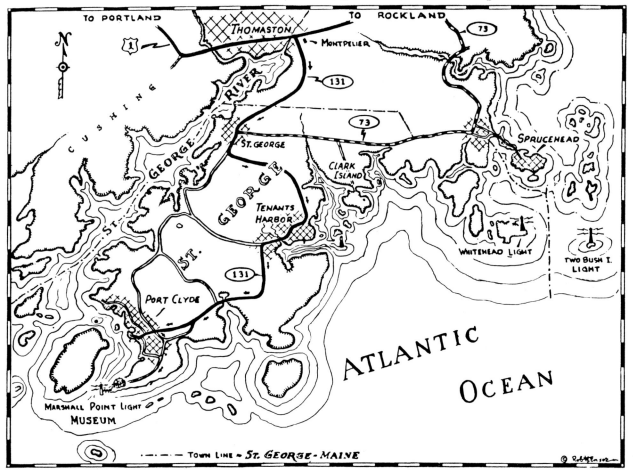